# TWO KINGS

Emma Lewis

A long time ago, and yet perhaps not such a long time ago after all,
an old king left this world for the next.

The old king had no children, so the job of ruler was suddenly available.
Nobody was sure who would take the throne.

Confident that he should be in charge, a vain earl wasted no time in crowning himself king.

To begin with the people accepted this so they could continue living in peace.
Besides, what good would come of arguing with an earl?

But the news soon reached a greedy duke who ruled a nearby land. He was quite certain that he was the rightful king. After all, he was already in charge of one country, so why not another?

Furious with the earl, the duke began to make plans to invade so as to claim
the crown and the kingdom for himself.

The duke was busy preparing for battle when a strange and beautiful star with a glittering tail appeared across the skies.

The people of the land were worried. This could only mean troubled times ahead.
Something had to be done.

A message was sent to persuade both the earl and the duke to settle the matter of who should be king without fighting. But the pleas of the people and the sign in the sky were ignored.

The duke prepared very carefully for war; not a thing was missed.
The people of the land became his army, and the land itself became their armour.

A stretch of deep, dark water was all that stood between the duke and the earl.

The duke and his army would have to cross it.

Meanwhile, the earl marched his troops through towns and fields to quickly reach the coast.

The people watched on helplessly, foreseeing the trouble that was to come.

As night fell, the duke and his soldiers safely reached the shore.

While they waited for the earl and his troops to arrive, they feasted.

When the sun rose again, the two mighty armies spotted each other.

The day of battle had come.

A cry of horns sounded, and echoed far across the land for all to hear.

Soldiers from both sides fell.

Before long, it was difficult to know who had been fighting who in the first place.

The war was fierce and terrible, but finally it came to an end.

The vanity of the earl and the greediness of the duke meant that they had destroyed each other.
Now neither would be king.

The people of the land looked around, bewildered at all that had been lost.
And so it was suggested, and everyone agreed, that the country could be rebuilt together.

The people took it in turns to share their ideas and their ways of life.
Everyone had a say, and everyone was listened to.

Eventually, the land took shape once again, different to before, but better.
It was named Battle, so that the pointlessness of war would never be forgotten.

The people marvelled at their shared nation and a grand parade was held to celebrate.
It was a parade like none had ever seen before.

At long last, peace had been restored to the people.

*"Peace is the only battle worth waging."* Albert Camus

For Joshua and Evy - E.L.

Two Kings is inspired by the artwork of the Bayeux Tapestry, an embroidered cloth over 70 metres long and 50 centimetres tall. It was created in the eleventh century and depicts the Battle of Hastings, one of the most momentous events in British history. Emma was inspired by the imagery and colours of the tapestry after seeing it while she was on holiday in France.

First published 2018 by order of the Tate Trustees
by Tate Publishing, a division of Tate Enterprises Ltd,
Millbank, London SW1P 4RG

www.tate.org.uk/publishing
Text and illustrations © Emma Lewis, 2018

ISBN 978 1 8 4976 596 1

Distributed in the United States and Canada by ABRAMS, New York
Library of Congress Control Number applied for
Printed in China by C&C Offset Printing Co., Ltd.
Colour reproduction by Evergreen Colour Management Co., Ltd.